For Alison and Nick

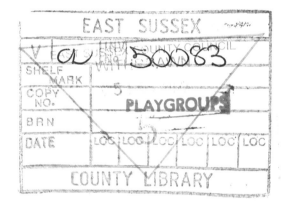

ORCHARD BOOKS
96 Leonard Street, London EC2A 4XD
Orchard Books, Australia
14 Mars Road, Lane Cove, NSW 2066
First published in Great Britain in 1990
This edition published in 1999
ISBN 1 84121 341 1 (hardback)
ISBN 1 84121 053 6 (paperback)
Text copyright © Laurence Anholt 1999
Illustrations copyright © Catherine Anholt 1990
The rights of Laurence Anholt to be identified as the author and
Catherine Anholt to be identified as the illustrator have been asserted
by them in accordance with the Copyright, Designs and Patents Act, 1988.
A CIP catalogue record for this book is available from the British Library
1 3 5 7 9 10 8 6 4 2 (hardback)
1 3 5 7 9 10 8 6 4 2 (paperback)
Printed in Singapore

Good Days Bad Days

Catherine and Laurence Anholt

ORCHARD BOOKS

In our
family

we have

good days

bad days

happy days

sad days

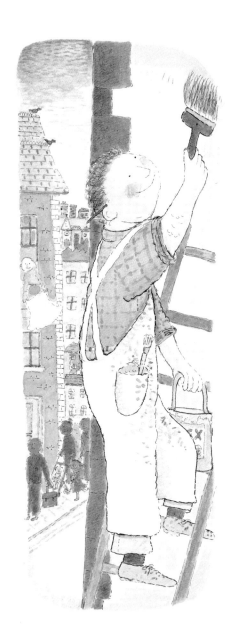

work days

play days

home days

away days

sunny days

snowy days

rainy days

blowy days

healthy days

sick days

slow days

quick days

school days

Sundays

dull days

fun days.

Every day's a different day

but the best day follows yesterday . . .

TODAY!